CLAYTON PARKER really Really REALLY has to PEE

Written by Cinco Paul

Illustrated by Gladys Jose

Abrams Books for Young Readers   New York

A boy named Clayton Parker from the town of Mountain View
was on a field trip headed for the San Francisco Zoo.

He hoped to see a tiger. A giraffe. A chimpanzee!

But Clayton Parker

REALLY REALLY
REALLY

had to pee.

The morning of the field trip, Clayton's teacher, Mrs. Howe, said, "If you have to go, my friends, the time to go is NOW."

But Clayton didn't have to go! He honestly did not!

And so he got onto the bus without a second thought.

But as the bus was bouncing up and down and to and fro,

poor Clayton felt that old familiar pressure down below.

Oh no! he thought.

Is that—?

Am I—?

I mean—but could it be?

Yes, Clayton Parker

really really

REALLY

had to pee.

See, when you drink some juice, let's say,
once it has left your mouth,

it goes down your esophagus
and keeps on heading

SOUTH.

HELLO
MY NAME IS
Dr. Bladder

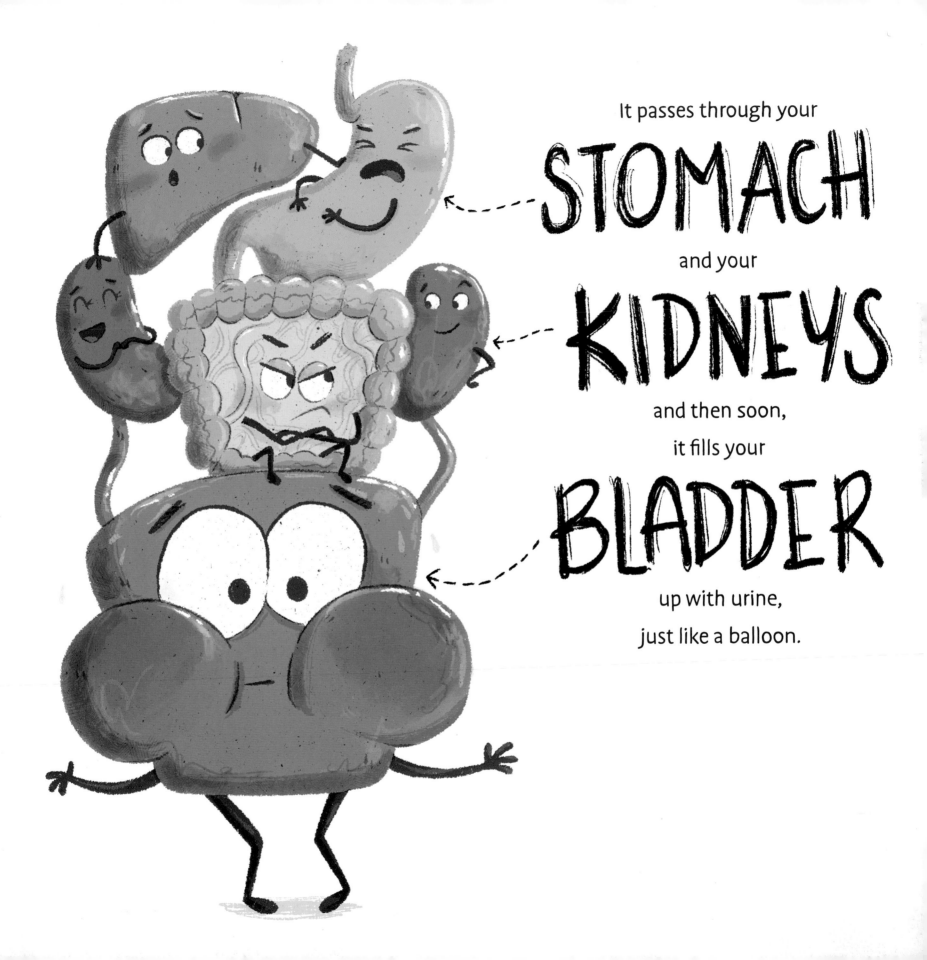

It passes through your

STOMACH

and your

KIDNEYS

and then soon,

it fills your

BLADDER

up with urine,

just like a balloon.

And then your bladder sends a message
way up to your brain

that says,
"HEY THERE! I'M FILLED WITH
ALL THE PEE I CAN CONTAIN!"

But Clayton didn't want a lesson in biology.

He only knew he really

really REALLY

had to pee.

And then, at last, the bus arrived—they'd made it to the zoo!

And little Clayton Parker knew just what he had to do.

He had to find a restroom,
and he had to find one fast—
because he wasn't certain
how much longer he could last.

He didn't want to end up
like a boy named David France,
who, years ago, in front of all the school,
had peed his PANTS.

No, Clayton did not want to make that kind of HISTORY.

But here's the thing: HE really really

REALLY HAD TO PEE.

The schoolkids all got off the bus and formed a single line
while Clayton started looking for that magic **"RESTROOM"** sign.

He saw one! So he ran to it, forgetting all his cares,

until he saw another sign, which read . . .

The **AGONY** that Clayton felt! He yearned to urinate!

He wondered: Am I **DOOMED** to suffer David France's fate?

He joined a tour and followed it and saw what he could see,
but Clayton Parker REALLY REALLY

REALLY

had to pee.

He spied a clump of bushes
and he wondered, *Do I dare?*

*Should I hide out behind them
and relieve my burden there?*

He started to attempt just that,
but then, to his surprise,

and
PLUMES
and
EYES!

He ran away, in deep despair!

His bladder 'bout to burst!

Would Clayton ever find relief? Or was the boy just cursed?

And what if he exploded?

What a nightmare that would be!

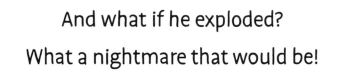

THE CHAOS!
THE CONFUSION!

Nothing left of him but pee!

But what was that? Was it a sign?
And did that sign say **MEN**?

Uncertain he could trust his eyes,
the boy looked up again.

It did! He'd finally found it!
Now he'd have to wait no more!

He hurdled three small children
as he barreled toward the door.

He stepped into the stall and then let nature take its course.

(I've heard his flow was like that of a massive Clydesdale horse!)

OUT OF ORDER

And while he did, young Clayton
vowed in all sincerity:

*Before I head
out anywhere,
I'll*
ALWAYS
try to pee.

He zipped his pants and washed his hands and made his way outside,

a new skip in his step, an added sureness to his stride.

He shouted

"HALLELUJAH!"

and he did a little dance . . .

until a nearby elephant sprayed water on his pants.

For Norma Paul, who always asked if I needed to go.

—C.P.

To every parent out there . . . you know why.

—G.J.

The art for this book was created with Adobe Photoshop and Fresco.

Library of Congress Cataloging-in-Publication Data
Names: Paul, Cinco, author. | Jose, Gladys, illustrator. Title: Clayton Parker really really really has to pee /
written by Cinco Paul ; illustrated by Gladys Jose. Description: New York, NY : Abrams Books for Young Readers, 2021. |
Audience: Ages 4–8. | Summary: Follows a young boy's desperate search to find a bathroom
while on a school field trip to the zoo.
Identifiers: LCCN 2020031306 | ISBN 9781419748639 (hardcover)
Subjects: CYAC: Stories in rhyme. | Urination—Fiction. | Zoos—Fiction. |
School field trips—Fiction. | Humorous stories.
Classification: LCC PZ8.3.P27366 Cl 2021 | DDC [E]—dc23
LC record available at https://lccn.loc.gov/2020031306

Text © 2021 Cinco Paul
Illustrations © 2021 Gladys Jose
Book design by Heather Kelly

Printed and bound in China
10 9 8 7 6 5 4 3 2 1

Abrams Books for Young Readers are available at special discounts when purchased in quantity for premiums and
promotions as well as fundraising or educational use. Special editions can also be created to specification.
For details, contact specialsales@abramsbooks.com or the address below.

Abrams® is a registered trademark of Harry N. Abrams, Inc.

ABRAMS The Art of Books
195 Broadway, New York, NY 10007
abramsbooks.com